THE
LADY FROM
NOWHERE

Cerberus Jones

Kane Miller
A DIVISION OF EDC PUBLISHING

CHAPTER ONE

Amelia was the last one out for lunch, still smearing on sunscreen and looking for her hat while the rest of class galloped out to the beach at the bottom of the school playground.

"Sorry, Ms. Slaviero," she said, trying to hurry.

"Got your lunch?" her teacher asked, cheerfully. "There's nothing better than the taste of sunscreen on your sandwiches, is there?"

Now that Amelia was ready, she really wanted to run and catch up with the others, but seeing as Ms. Slaviero had been nice enough to wait, she felt obliged to walk with her.

But why do adults always have to go so slowly? At this rate, she'd miss the end of lunch as well as the beginning. And from the sound of it, something awesome was going on.

As she and Ms. Slaviero trudged between the sand dunes, following the little slatted path from the school to Forgotten Bay Beach, she could hear Charlie shouting above the excited voices of the other kids. She itched to sprint the last stretch.

"Go on," laughed Ms. Slaviero. "I'll be right behind you."

She pelted as fast as she could over the last rise and down to the beach. She could see her classmates all gathered on the other side of the storm water creek, at the foot of the lighthouse headland.

"Ugh, don't touch it, Erik," Sophie T. was saying. "It stinks."

Through the crowd of children, Amelia could

see something gray and pinkish lying on the sand. She couldn't tell what it was, but it was big. She saw a broad, shallow trench through the sand coming up from the water's edge, as though the thing had crawled from the ocean.

"It's a sea monster," said Callan.

"Don't be silly," said Shani. "There's no such thing. But it could be a genetically mutated fish."

Amelia's eyes widened. Monsters? Mutants? *Oh no* – she ran over to the kids and pushed her way into the circle surrounding the thing. She looked first at it, and then at Charlie.

What is that?

Clearly it was dead, and just as clearly, most of it had been eaten away, leaving nothing but a strange, rubbery, gray skeleton. Could it be an alien of some sort?

For months now, Amelia and Charlie (and more recently, Sophie T.) had been keeping it a secret that Amelia's home, the Gateway Hotel on the other side of the bay, was actually home to a gateway across *space*, bringing in alien visitors from all over the universe.

But what good was it to keep a secret if those aliens were leaving the hotel's grounds and getting themselves eaten on the beach where anyone could see?

She looked over to Charlie again, but he was gone.

"I'm telling you," Callan was still going on, "it's a baby kraken. It probably got sick from the ocean's acid levels rising."

"Or a shark," Charlie called from somewhere.

"I doubt it," said Callan. "I mean, look at the size of this spine! Plus –"

"No, really," Charlie interrupted. Amelia saw his head grinning over a pile of sand. He was waving a stick to get their attention. "I just found the head. It's a great white shark for sure."

Amelia and the rest hurried over and saw that

Charlie was standing in a kind of pit in the sand. By his feet was the huge, blunt head of what was undoubtedly a shark. Not an alien. But then –

She looked back at the trough carved through the sand from the shoreline.

Drag marks, she realized. *And this hole in the ground didn't just get here by itself.*

Something had caught a great white shark the length of the school's minibus, hauled it uphill through the sand, eaten the whole thing down to its cartilage skeleton, and then dug a hole deep enough to bury it. She guessed that the *something* had been disturbed and run off, leaving the evidence behind.

But what could be powerful enough to do all that, but still be bothered enough by humans to hide?

She had a sinking feeling, and then someone tugged at her elbow.

"Look," Sophie T. whispered, and pointed at some footprints in the sand.

The prints were blurred up here where the sand was powdery, but if you were looking for them, and if you already suspected enough to guess what it was you were seeing ...

Amelia looked at Sophie T.

"Grawk," they said together.

Her alien "dog." His species were fearsome predators on their home planet, and here on Earth, he'd grown supersized. At least this explained how he'd been feeding himself. Amelia gazed at the long, beautiful curve of the bay. How many other enormous skeletons had Grawk buried under the sand?

"Hello, hello," Ms. Slaviero puffed, arriving at last. "What's all the excitement?"

"Dead shark!" Shani called. "Charlie found the head."

"Ooh, good job, kids. Have you identified the type?"

"It's a great white," Charlie said proudly, and

then added, "you should see the teeth."

Amelia wondered how to get rid of the paw prints without anyone noticing what she was doing, but Sophie T. just pulled her back toward the rest of the group.

"Ignore them," she hissed to Amelia. "No one else will see unless we point it out."

Amelia didn't like that, but she couldn't think of an alternative.

"Trust me," Sophie T. shuddered. "Nobody, not even Callan, really wants to know the truth. Just come and listen to Ms. Slaviero and act like nothing's wrong."

Amelia went back to the group, and saw that Sophie T. was right. Ms. Slaviero had everyone's attention.

"Did you know great whites are born live from their mother's bodies?" she was saying with gruesome relish. "The eggs hatch inside her, and she carries the babies for about eleven months.

And what do you think they eat while they're in there? *Each other.*"

"Eww!" The kids all writhed in disgust, and Sophie T. gave Amelia a knowing look.

Amelia smiled back, but her heart wasn't in it. True, they'd gotten away with this incident, this time, for now – but what about the next one? And the next?

It seemed like the harder Amelia, Charlie and their families tried to protect the secrets of the gateway, the more determined they were to break out.

The next morning, Amelia banged on a guest room door halfway down the hallway from hers.

"I'm up," she heard Charlie yawn. "I'm coming."

Charlie's mum, Mary, had gone out for dinner the night before, so he'd slept over even though it was a school night. He'd slept over so often lately that the Walkers had offered Charlie one of the guest rooms in the Gateway Hotel to have as his own. Charlie, of course, had accepted immediately. He'd been ready to move in from the day he'd first met Tom (the grumpy, one-eyed caretaker) and seen the overgrown hedge maze in the grounds – it was the real haunted hotel everyone in Forgotten Bay thought it was.

At first, Amelia's parents had been able to change people's minds about that. They'd restored the hotel nearly to its original state, and made it a popular retreat for tourists and vacationers. It was a beautiful old place, standing proudly at the top of the headland with amazing views of the ocean all around. And there was the peculiar fact that electronic devices didn't work up there because of the magnetic field put out by the cave system that ran underneath it all.

"Charmingly old-fashioned," Mum called it in the ads she had run in the papers. And heaps of people had agreed. Until Krskn, the Guild's most infamous, cruel and dangerous mercenary, had arrived last week.

Amelia still didn't know much about the Guild – but she did know they were ancient and powerful, and that it had taken an interstellar war to free the gateway network from their grip.

She also knew they were making a comeback.

Disguised by a crystal-powered holo-emitter, Krskn had stolen a canister so secret not even Control knew about it. Nobody really knew what was in the canister, but as Amelia had found out the hard way, it made the gateway violently sick.

Trying to escape Earth with the canister, Krskn had dragged Amelia through the gateway as his hostage, nearly killing them both. The resulting catastrophe had blasted through the whole cave system, smashing out the hidden trapdoor in the library and filling the hotel with sand, glowing lichen, and a plague of tiny, vicious alien bats.

On one hand, it had been a great victory for Control. Krskn had been arrested, and was even now safely in custody at Control's Earth headquarters, and the Guild had been thwarted again. On the other hand, it was the closest they'd come yet to complete disaster. Ms. Rosby – one of the top three Control agents on Earth – had somehow managed to smooth things over with the thirty human guests who'd been staying at the time, but Control had had enough. No more human guests were to come to the headland. The existence of aliens had to be hidden.

All of which meant there were suddenly plenty of empty bedrooms for Charlie to choose from. He emerged from his room looking rumpled, and he and Amelia skipped down the marble staircase to the lobby. Mum was scowling to herself, the old landline phone to her ear.

"Shh!" Amelia pointed it out to Charlie.

"Don't worry," said Mum, hanging up with a

bang. "The wretched thing's out – not even a dial tone."

Amelia grimaced in sympathy, and followed Charlie down the hall to the staff room to have breakfast and make their lunch for school.

She opened the pantry – and leaped back with a shout of alarm as a yellow object flew into her face, screeching. Charlie laughed as she swiped at the alien bat, swatting it aside. It staggered in midair before fluttering off drunkenly, defeated.

Amelia shot Charlie a cold stare.

"What?" Charlie protested. "That was a good shot. You've got ninja reflexes."

Amelia said nothing.

"That's a compliment," Charlie explained. "Relax. I'm being *nice*."

"Nice?" Amelia shook her head at him. "Every single one of those bats, every time they attack me in the shower, or from under the dining table, or inside my schoolbag, or a million other places,

I feel as though I'm right back in that wormhole, being kidnapped by Krskn, thinking I'm going to die. So, no, I can't relax. And I don't know how you can."

"Listen, I was scared too. I just –" Charlie shrugged. "I can't keep on being so anxious all the time. It's *exhausting*. Plus, everything's okay now, right? Krskn's in jail, and the canister is finally gone, and –"

"It's not *gone*," Amelia interrupted. "It's *lost*. Krskn didn't get it, but neither did we, so no, everything is not okay. Not until we know that thing is safe."

"Good point," said Charlie. "Come on, then."

He walked out of the staff room and headed for the library, slapping away two more micro-bats that ambushed him from the doorway.

"What are you doing?" asked Amelia, following.

"I thought you wanted to find out about the canister," said Charlie, stopping outside the door. "I've been thinking: Tom said it had been hidden in the safe in your room since long before his time, so we know it's old. And we know it's secret, but maybe we'll find something here to help us understand it. There's got to be *something* good in here, right?"

"Maybe." Amelia was dubious. "But later. Come on, we're going to be late for –"

But at that moment, a thump sounded from inside the library. Amelia and Charlie turned to look at each other – and then pulled open the door and slipped inside.

They could hear unsteady footsteps from across the room, out of the secret stairway in the library annex. The sliding panel that was meant to hide the annex from the library proper had been broken in the gateway explosion, as had the trapdoor in the floor beyond. And now someone was coming through.

Despite his bravado earlier, Charlie paled. And

despite her jumpiness and expectation of the worst, Amelia ran straight over to the annex to investigate.

"Leaf Man!" she exclaimed, seeing the tall, black-coated man trudging up the steps.

He was painfully thin, but Amelia knew he was strong enough to lift her and Charlie off the ground, one in each hand, without any apparent effort. But now he was bent double under the weight of one little old lady who was slumped over his shoulders in a fireman's hold.

Either the woman was far, far heavier than she looked, or –

"Help her," Leaf Man said weakly, and collapsed to his knees, trying not to drop the woman, but only seconds away from passing out.

Amelia and Charlie rushed to break Leaf Man's fall, and between them, they gently lowered the unconscious alien to the floor. They pulled the apparently human woman from Leaf Man's back and laid her beside him, turning her on her side like Ms. Slaviero had taught them in first aid.

Amelia gasped in shock. She recognized the woman immediately, but not from having met her before. She knew her from a painting – a portrait that had been hanging in her bedroom when they'd first moved into the hotel. A portrait that, according to her dad, had been painted nearly one hundred and fifty years ago.

Matilda Swervingthorpe, the original owner of the Gateway Hotel.

CHAPTER TWO

"Told you we'd find something good in here," said Charlie, staring.

Amelia reeled back and yelled out the door toward the lobby, "Help! Someone? We need help!"

Then she crouched beside the two collapsed figures on the annex floor, and tried to remember some of the first aid Ms. Slaviero had taught them. She used two fingers (*not* her thumb) to check Matilda Swervingthorpe's pulse. The old lady's heartbeat was steady, and her chest rose and fell evenly – as far as Amelia could tell, she was uninjured. Amelia didn't know what else to do with her, so she moved on to Leaf Man and felt the side of his neck.

"What's up?" said Charlie, seeing her frown.

"He's really cold, and ..." She checked the other side of his neck, and then both his wrists. "His holo-emitter's there, but – I can't find a pulse."

"He's *dead?*"

Amelia bit her lip. "I don't know. I never asked him if he usually has a pulse. Maybe he doesn't even have a heart."

"And he's always that chalky white," Charlie mused. "Maybe he's a vampire."

Amelia glared at him, too worried for jokes. She heard heavy footsteps thumping through the lobby, and a second later her older brother, James, ran into the library.

"Amelia! What's wrong? Where are –" He came through the annex door, and halted abruptly. "What happened?" he asked, shocked.

"Leaf Man came up through the tunnels carrying the old lady," said Charlie. "She was out cold already, and he collapsed as soon as he got up here."

"Okay. And who is she?"

"Matilda Swervingthorpe," said Amelia. If she said it enough, it would start to sound true, right?

James balked. "Don't be silly. She only looks about seventy years old. If it were really her she'd have to be –"

"Over two hundred years old," Amelia finished. "I know, but it *is* her. She looks exactly like the portrait from my room, and check it out – she's even wearing the same horrible hat."

"Not possible," said James. "It's probably just –"

"It's not a holo-emitter," Amelia said severely. "I would've found it when I was checking her pulse. Anyway, who cares? We need to help them. We can work out who she is, and how it's all possible, after we know they're okay."

James grimaced at himself and nodded in agreement with his sister. "Okay, okay, you're right. Although I don't really know what we can do for them."

"Well, where's Mum and Dad, then?"

James, kneeling down beside Matilda Swervingthorpe, patted her cheek gently to see if it had any effect. "Mum went to find Dad to sort out the phones. I think Tom's still down at Control HQ. He had that early morning meeting with Ms. Rosby, remember?"

"I've got it!" said Charlie suddenly. "Matilda Swervingthorpe was in suspended animation, or cryo-sleep or something! That's why she hasn't aged."

Amelia rolled her eyes in frustration, but James was right on it.

"No such thing," said James. "That's just in movies. In real life, the Guild – I mean the ancient Guild, before they found the gateway and went power mad and evil – spent their whole lives traveling across space. It took generations of families to make a single voyage, and you've got to believe they would have used hibernation technology if they could."

"Well, she wasn't on a starship, was she?" Charlie said stubbornly. "Obviously, she got lost through a wormhole."

"Oh!" James's face lit up with understanding. "That's it!"

Charlie grinned.

"I mean, she didn't go through a wormhole, that's totally wrong. But what if she fell *between* wormholes?" James was so excited by his own train of thought, he seemed to have forgotten the two unconscious people beside him. He rattled on, "She would have landed in the Nowhere. And from what I can tell from talking to Tom, it isn't *nothing* at all. It's the opposite: the place where all the dimensions exist at once."

"Like Earth, then," said Charlie.

"No," said James, his eyes glazed with wonder. "Here we only live in three dimensions – or four, if you count time. But the Nowhere has *ten* dimensions. At least. Space would work completely differently there. So time would, too. For a human being, it might be as if time didn't exist at all."

"Right," Amelia jumped in. "Like this human being right here in front of us."

James, startled, looked down at Matilda Swervingthorpe. "Right. Her."

"I wonder why Leaf Man only brought her back now," said Charlie. "A bit slack of him to make her wait."

"Well," said James, "of course, from her point of view, there wouldn't have been a wait at all –"

"He didn't make her wait," said Amelia. "Last time we saw Leaf Man, he told Tom the canister had stirred up the Nowhere, and revealed a clue of where to look for someone. All this time, she must have been lost, even from Leaf Man."

"*Her?*" said Charlie, pointing. "How would she know –"

But at that exact moment *she* heaved in a huge breath, sat bolt upright and screamed, "Get your hands off me, you filthy convicts!"

Amelia and James stared at her, speechless, and Charlie hastily dropped his pointing finger.

Matilda Swervingthorpe blinked at the three of them, put both hands to her face as if to check she was in the right body, and then looked at the room around her, frowning and alarmed. When she saw Leaf Man lying unconscious beside her, she scrambled to her feet (a little stiffly) and demanded of James, "What have you done to him?"

"Me? What? Nothing!" he stammered.

"Then what's wrong with him? And what happened to me?" Matilda spoke imperiously, like she was used to bossing people around and getting her own way, but Amelia saw her hands trembling by her side.

Matilda looked around the annex, her face thunderous as she took in the smashed trapdoor, the ruined walls and the drifts of sand and cave lichen that nobody had gotten around to cleaning up yet.

"What have you done to my house? Who let you in? And apart from all that, why haven't any of you got your clothes on?"

"Hey!" Charlie was indignant, but Amelia tried to see it from Matilda's point of view. Matilda was wearing a dress that buttoned right up to her chin, with long sleeves, and a skirt that fell in heavy, layered ruffles over an enormous bustle so that she almost looked like the front half of a (well-dressed) horse costume. On top of her head perched an equally complicated hat, all ribbons and feathers, with a huge green stone brooch

pinned on the front. Compared to that, their school T-shirts and shorts must have made them look practically naked.

"It's okay," Amelia said soothingly. "You're safe. Whatever happened before, it's over now."

Matilda looked at her sharply. "What do you know about what happened before?"

"Er ..."

"Exactly," she snapped. "So how can you stand there in your underthings and assure me it's over? You're trespassing on my land, and from how you've treated my library, I can see you're barbarians. My advice to you is to pack up your things and be gone from here in the next quarter of an hour."

"Or what?" said Charlie.

"Or you will see things," Matilda said darkly, "that will make you wish you'd never been born."

She let the words hang in the air and drew herself up, staring at them impressively. Amelia,

James and Charlie all looked at one another, not sure how to break it to her.

"Um, excuse me, Matilda," Amelia said, being as polite as she could. Which was not nearly polite enough: the old woman's nostrils flared.

"I mean, Miss Swervingthorpe," Amelia hurried on. "It's been ... er," she looked at James.

He nodded. "Well, you've been gone a long time. Long enough that, um ... we live here now."

Amelia winced, waiting for the inevitable angry outburst, but to her surprise, Matilda seemed to relax for the first time since she'd regained consciousness. She looked Amelia up and down and considered her short-cropped hair with apparent fascination.

"I see," she said at last. "How long, may I ask?"

Amelia hesitated. She remembered the story of Rip Van Winkle and how distressed he'd been to learn he'd slept away twenty years on the mountainside.

 27

But Charlie blurted out, "About a hundred and forty years."

Matilda stepped back, her eyes wide, then bit her lip and frowned, thinking hard. And then she smiled.

"Sterling! A hundred and forty years and the old place is still here. And yet –" She stopped, then said in a bright, careless voice, "Children, will you humor an old lady? I have such a silly, funny question to ask you, but are you – the three of you – really human beings?"

"As human as you are," said Charlie.

Matilda narrowed her eyes at him. "And how human is that, dear?"

"Exactly," said Charlie. "You tell us."

The two of them glared at each other for several uncomfortable moments, and Amelia was struck by how bizarrely similar the two faces were. They could hardly have looked less alike, and yet they were perfectly matched in belligerence.

Suddenly, Matilda laughed out loud and clapped her hands. "So you know about the fairy portal, then? Bravo!"

"The gateway?" said James. "Yeah, that's why we're here."

"And the demons? They're gone?"

Amelia's mind raced. She could see how a person from the 1870s might think of the wormhole travelers as fairies or demons rather than intergalactic aliens, but which demons was Matilda talking about?

"We don't know much about your time here," Amelia said. "We don't even know why you went missing. We only guessed it must have been the gateway."

Matilda looked down at Leaf Man, still immobile on the floor. "If only my dear Horatio were awake, I'm sure he could explain it all to me in an instant."

"Horatio?" Charlie laughed.

"It's better than Leaf Man," Amelia pointed out.

"So you know him?" said James.

"Of course." Matilda smiled fondly. "It was I who gave him that trench coat he's still wearing, though it was in rather better condition at the time. And he, in return, gave me this jewel." She reached up and touched the hideous green brooch on the front of her hat.

"Er, how nice," said Amelia.

Matilda laughed. "Oh, it's a true horror, isn't it? Everyone in town thought I'd gone doolally when I started wearing it. Every day, no matter my dress, even when I was in my painting smock, I always wore Horatio's gem."

"You must really treasure it," Amelia said, trying to be kind.

Matilda gave her a quizzical look. "Treasure it, my dear? Oh, no – it was quite a malicious joke, to give me something so brutally ugly. I laughed like a drain when he gave it to me."

Amelia was intrigued. Matilda and Leaf Man had obviously been very good friends – close enough not just to give each other gifts, but joke presents.

"Anyway," Matilda went on, "it wasn't given to me as decoration. This was Horatio's way of arming me."

"It's a weapon?" Charlie asked.

"A weapon of a kind. It somehow collects information. I think it's something like a wax cylinder for recording sound, or a silver plate for making photographs, only rather more wonderful."

"Oh!" James unconsciously reached out for the green stone. "It must be something like the crystals they use in the holo-emitters. May I have a look?"

Matilda drew back, considering. "Perhaps. Once I know who all of *you* are."

"Who's there?" Dad's voice echoed through the empty lobby. "Amelia? Charlie? School starts in ten minutes! You guys are almost –" He stopped in the library doorway, and gawped at Matilda.

"Out of time?" Charlie suggested.

CHAPTER THREE

Dad shook hands with Matilda in utter delight. He couldn't take his eyes off her, but when he spoke it was to James.

"She was in the Nowhere?"

"Yep."

"We were right, mate! By crikey, what I wouldn't give to be able to talk about this with those string theory guys back at the Institute!"

"Scott?"

"Oh!" Dad dropped Matilda's hand and turned to call back through the doorway, "In here, Skye. We've got a visitor."

Matilda skewered him with a look.

"Sorry," Dad called out to Mum again. "Scratch that – *we're* the visitors."

"What are you on about?" Mum came in, smiling. There was a split second of shock when she saw Matilda, but almost immediately, she squared her shoulders, straightened her spine, and gave a very pretty curtsy. "Miss Swervingthorpe," she said politely, as though *of course* she was meeting a woman who'd been lost, and presumed dead, for a century and a half. "I'm sorry your house is so unpresentable for your return."

Matilda nodded in approval (though Amelia did see her taking in Mum's jeans with alarm).

"What happened to the Keeper?" Mum asked.

"Just exhausted, we hope," said Amelia. "He carried Ma – Miss Swervingthorpe up here and then sort of fainted."

Dad looked down at the unconscious alien and rubbed his hands together with glee. "What must all those dimensions be like? Ah, what he could tell us!"

Matilda looked at him sternly. "Horatio risked his life to bring me back, sir. He didn't do it to satisfy your curiosity." Then she turned to Mum. "Is my bedroom as I left it, by any chance?"

Mum shook her head, and seemed to understand what Matilda was really asking. "The canister is gone, I'm afraid."

Matilda paled. "And we're standing here making conversation? Are you lunatics? There's not a second to spare!"

"The Guild don't have it," said Charlie. "They tried to steal it, but we stopped them. Twice."

"Then *where is it?*" Matilda's voice was cold.

"Gone," said Amelia. "At least – we thought at first it was lost down in the caves, but Lady Naomi scanned for it – it's nowhere on the whole headland."

Matilda sniffed. "Then we must search *beyond*

35

the headland – and we must begin at once, before the demons return."

But Amelia had remembered something. "Dad, Miss Swervingthorpe's gem is a recording device. Leaf Man gave it to her."

"Fantastic! Can you show us what you've got?"

Matilda shook her head. "I'm afraid Horatio never explained the contraption to me. He seemed to think it safer that way."

"We can probably figure it out, Dad," said James. "If it's the same tech as the holo-emitters, it shouldn't take us long."

"No," said Dad. "Whatever's on here, we can't risk accidentally erasing the data."

"What about Tom?" said Charlie.

"He's still at Control," Mum reminded him. "And with the phones out, we can't easily call him back, or ask if anyone there can help us."

Dad looked at the unconscious Leaf Man and shook his head. "We couldn't ask Control anyway.

The Keeper wanted everything about the canister kept secret, and we have to assume this data is included. I think we should ask Lady Naomi first, and hope the Keeper recovers in the meantime."

Even though everyone wanted to act immediately, there was still some delay. Amelia and Charlie kept very quiet, in case someone remembered that they should be at school, but it was maddening. Matilda wouldn't let anyone touch the brooch, and insisted on carrying it herself to Lady Naomi, but there was no way she could make the trek through the bush in that huge dress.

"For pity's sake," she snapped at last. "Just get me a pair of those obscene breeches you're all wearing and let's go."

So, after some digging around in Mum's closet, they were finally on their way, Matilda still wearing her horrendous hat, but now in Mum's gardening pants, a pair of Amelia's sneakers, and a flannel shirt. She looked ridiculous, but had no vanity at all. She just wanted to get going.

Leaving Mum with Leaf Man, Dad, James, Amelia, Charlie and Matilda set out across the hotel's lawn, heading for the bush track beyond the hedge maze.

"So tell me," said Dad, as they swished through the long grass. "How did you come to work for the Keeper?"

"I didn't work for him. We were friends, and then comrades in arms. I didn't exert myself for *money.*"

"Right, well." Amelia could hear Dad struggling to ask the next question. He didn't get things like manners and protocol the way Mum did; he just wanted the info.

Amelia piped up, trying to help. "You built such a beautiful house, Miss Swervingthorpe. How did you come to live in Forgotten Bay?"

Matilda's eyes gleamed. "Ah, surely you guessed. The magnetism! Although I trained as an artist, my real passion is magneto-therapy. I searched the world and spent half my inheritance before I found this natural marvel of a headland. I bought it knowing that living in such a powerful magnetic field would rejuvenate me, and I would never get old or ill."

Amelia saw James choking back a guffaw, and heard Dad mutter "quackery" in disgust, but Matilda went on.

"It took fifteen years to build the house, and then I was here another twenty after that, and I knew Horatio for almost all that time. Oh, what a beauty he is! What elegance, what grace, what extraordinary coloring! The first time I saw him cutting across my land, I introduced myself and begged him to let me paint him."

Amelia and Charlie swapped puzzled looks. Could she really be talking about *their* Leaf Man?

Skinny, shabby Leaf Man with his shaggy black hair and dead-white face?

Charlie shrugged. "Artists ..."

"And so you were friends?" Amelia prompted.

"Yes. And then, when I got to know him better, I realized he was deeply afraid of something. When I asked him, he told me about the demons."

"And the gateway?" said Charlie. "Did he tell you about that?"

"Oh, I discovered that for myself, of course."

James held aside the leaves of the banksia tree whose leaning trunk hid the start of Lady Naomi's path through the bush, and Matilda ducked underneath.

"The first thing I did when I bought the place was look for the source of the magnetism. It didn't take long to discover that the headland's treasure lay in its cave system. Even before the house was built, I had set up a laboratory in one cavern, and put my bed in a delightful little fairy grotto filled with pink glowing lichen. There wasn't anything that happened in those caves – no strange gusts of exotic air or groaning shift in the ether – that I didn't know about and record.

"Over the months I watched dozens of elfin creatures coming and going through the fairy portal. Delightful little things, bringing boxes and containers one day, disappearing with them the next, always busy and serious, and quite charming. But the demons were something else."

They were quiet as they walked around the last bend in the path and then into the clearing where Lady Naomi's workstation stood. She'd been out here every day since Krskn's arrest, no longer scanning the skies for her home planet, but trying to repair the damage he'd done to her equipment so she could scan again for the canister, looking wider with each sweep.

"Lady Naomi!" Dad called. "Come and meet someone extraordinary."

Lady Naomi spun around in surprise, but her face hardened when she saw Matilda, and she waited for them with her arms crossed. Even though Krskn was now in custody at Control headquarters, she'd plainly had enough of miraculous surprise gateway visitors. She wasn't about to let herself be fooled again.

"We need your help," Dad went on, oblivious. "The Keeper brought Miss Swervingthorpe here back from the Nowhere, and she has with her some kind of crystal data recorder he gave her, but she doesn't know how to use it."

Lady Naomi raised her eyebrows. "So ask the Keeper."

"He's unconscious," said Charlie.

"Uh-huh," Lady Naomi eyed Matilda, skeptical. "That's convenient."

"It *is* her," said Amelia. "Before he fainted, Leaf Man asked us to help her. And *she* was unconscious then – no way was she forcing him to say it."

"*She* is right here, madam," said Matilda.

"Sorry," said Amelia, then to Lady Naomi, "Can you help us see her recordings?"

Lady Naomi sighed. "I'll do my best. But we all know now that images can be faked, right?"

"I've never faked anything in my life," snapped Matilda. "I resent the accusation!"

"I bet," said Lady Naomi, her face expressionless. "So. The recorder?"

Matilda glared at her, but Dad just plucked the hat off her head and handed it to Lady Naomi.

"It's the green stone in the brooch."

Lady Naomi looked at it carefully from all angles, and then took the brooch off the hat. Turning it over, she popped the stone free and rubbed it between her fingers.

"I've got my holo-screen back up and working, so I can amplify images and sound, but I won't be able to run a full diagnostic on when or where the images were made."

She was sour as she said this, but Amelia knew it was because she was angry with herself. These were exactly the tests she should have run on the images Krskn used to trick her.

"But how will your computer access the files?" asked James. "You don't even know where the stone came from, do you?"

"Compatibility is an Earth issue," said Lady Naomi, and flicked on her holo-screen. A huge black rectangle was projected in front of them and then the jewel glowed as she laid it in a tray beside the keyboard.

The screen lit up with a horrifying close-up of the multifaceted eyes of an insect. They glittered a weird, silvery blue, and it chittered through sticky black mandibles.

"Aargh!" Charlie recoiled in disgust. "No wonder you call them demons!"

"Demon?" said Matilda. "That's my Horatio."

The image panned back and they could see

more of the insect's body. Two of its hairy legs were raised and reaching out to the sides of the screen, and Amelia realized that the alien was putting the brooch on Matilda's hat. This really was Leaf Man in his true form.

"Are you sure about this?" he said in the recording.

"Quite," came Matilda's voice, louder than his because she was right under the stone. "I didn't like the look of those ruffians even before you told me about them. And they ignore me utterly – treat me like you would a half-tame kangaroo that keeps hanging around your veranda. They think I'm amusing, but harmless, and won't suspect a thing if they catch me hanging around the caverns."

"I don't like asking you –"

"You're not," Matilda interrupted, crisp and determined. "Now trust me. I'll find out what they're doing."

Lady Naomi fast-forwarded through Matilda's long trek through the tunnels and caverns to the gateway (all done by the light of a kerosene lamp) until she got to a massive chamber with many thick pillars. It was, Amelia realized, the place that had become the underground hotel – a sealed section of the caves that could be flooded with water for aquatic alien guests. But back in Matilda's day, it was being used as a warehouse for the Guild's trade. The holo-screen showed dozens of aliens, all of different species, carrying boxes here and there, and what was clearly a foreman in the middle, directing.

Then there was a flurry of activity. Some workers scurried away, others hustled into position behind the foreman. A second or two later, another alien entered the cavern. It was no taller than the others, but so squarely built, so heavily muscled, and covered with rough, reddish skin, with five horns across its brow and a short, pointed tail twitching behind, that Amelia knew it must have been one of Matilda's so-called "demons."

It barked at the foreman, and immediately three or four workers ran off. They returned with a lacquered black box, which they set at the demon's feet. The image shifted as Matilda crept closer. A couple of workers tried to shoo her away, but she just started humming a little song to herself and ignored them until they gave up and left her alone.

A half-tame kangaroo! Amelia smiled to herself. The old lady was gutsy all right.

The demon bent down and Matilda was close enough for the stone to capture him pulling an object out of the box that Amelia and Charlie instantly recognized: the canister!

"But how did they get it through the gateway?" Amelia wondered. "It nearly blew up when Krskn tried to leave with it."

"They didn't," said Matilda. "Whatever it is, it's been here in the caves long before the Guild arrived. Horatio knew about it, but could never go near enough to see what it was. The Guild only managed to bottle it up."

The demon put the canister back and yelled at his foreman a bit more.

"You can race through this part," said Matilda. "Go on, girl – giddy it up like you did before."

Lady Naomi looked at her sideways, but fast-forwarded. Amelia saw Matilda leave the caves, wander through the hotel, then blackness – perhaps her hat was in a cupboard? – then back down to the caves and – alarming even at this comical speed – Matilda sneaking past the workers and stealing the canister out of its lacquer box. She went back to the hotel and out to the hedge maze.

"Stop here," said the real Matilda. "Watch this bit in normal time."

The holo-screen showed Leaf Man arriving in his human form.

"Did you see it?" he asked abruptly. "Can you describe to me where to find it?"

"I can do better than that!" Matilda's voice was proud. "I can give it to you this instant!" Her hand appeared at the bottom of the screen, holding out the canister to Leaf Man.

He leaped back, shocked.

"Are you mad? They could have killed you!"

"I'm perfectly sane, and I took this without a single elf or gnome noticing me. And you needn't fear the substance – I've had this bottle on me for hours now and I haven't felt a thing. It's perfectly safe."

Leaf Man stretched out a hand, hesitant, but then he reeled back, and before Matilda could react, he'd collapsed to the ground.

"You can skip the next bit," the real Matilda snapped, and Amelia saw how pained she was to see Leaf Man's suffering. "Yes, yes, you can see the safe being installed in my bedroom, yes, there's me locking it away, go on, go on, back down to the fairy portal, and then – no, watch this part."

The same demon was in the warehouse cavern, and this time he had another three of his kind with him. They were carrying between them a beautiful curved object about the size of a guitar, a complicated arrangement of whorls and crescents in some sort of black stone that was obviously precious enough that it warranted a four-person escort.

"Oh, for the love of Mike Faraday," Dad gasped.

"What is it?" said Charlie.

"Shh!" hissed Lady Naomi. "Listen."

The demons were ordering the workers around, laughing with each other, and then shouting some more.

"You understand them?" said James.

Lady Naomi nodded. "It's just Chankrete –

standard trading language between planets. But this is worse than we thought. Oh, and now they're saying they want the canister – I suppose you know that?"

"My word, I do," said Matilda, grimly. She turned away from the screen.

Amelia and the rest watched helplessly as the black lacquer box was presented to the demons and found empty. There were ghastly howls of fury from the demons, shrieks of fear from the workers, and then the head demon spied Matilda. He shouted, and suddenly every alien in the warehouse was staring at her. A second after that, they were after her.

They heard Matilda breathing heavily, trying gamely to hum her idiotic little tune, trying to wander off casually, and then panicking and running for her life. She stumbled over her long skirts, but gathered them up. The images on the holo-screen were jerky and out of focus as

Matilda desperately darted in and out of rows of boxes, panting hard as she saw she was being driven closer to the gateway.

The aliens shouted at her, and she shouted back, "I don't understand!" More shouting, and then Matilda turned and leaped and the image flickered out.

She'd fallen into the Nowhere.

A moment later, the video resumed. Leaf Man's face filled the screen again. There was a sudden jerk, as though Matilda had been flipped upside down, and then nothing but a bumpy view of the cave floor as skinny insect legs scuttled over it. Amelia heard Leaf Man's ragged breath as he carried her out of the caves and realized that they were now watching footage that had been recorded today. A hundred and forty years had just flashed past with only the barest of blips in the recording.

Lady Naomi switched the holo-screen off.

"What were the aliens yelling?" Amelia asked.

"*Victory,*" Lady Naomi said tonelessly, still staring at the space where the holo-screen had been. "*Total control of the gateway is ours, as soon as we load the component into the manipulator.*"

"Control the gateway?" James was pale. "But they couldn't – surely they know how dangerous trying to harness the gateway would be?"

"Of course they do," said Lady Naomi, looking at him bleakly. "But the danger doesn't seem to have deterred them. And if that's what they were trying to do back then, I think we can guess that's exactly what they're trying to do now. They must have had time by now to build another manipulator."

"They don't need to build another one," said Dad, finally finding his voice. "The first one is still right here, waiting for them."

CHAPTER FOUR

"The manipulator is *here?*" Matilda gasped.

"Well, not *here* here," said Dad. "Not at the hotel. But it's here on Earth. In the boardroom at Control's headquarters."

"But why?" said Amelia.

"Well, you saw it on the screen, and believe me, it's even more impressive when you see it up close. Really a work of art. And because nobody could figure out what it was for, or if it did anything at all, they decided that it was probably just that: a work of art. Just a trophy from the victory over the Guild."

"Okay, so Control didn't know what they had," said James.

"Which is way dumb," Charlie interjected. "Since when were the Guild putting on art shows? Control should have known it was a weapon! They might not have known what the thing was, but they knew the Guild – they *knew* they were crazy evil."

James scowled at the interruption, and went on, "But even if Control didn't know what the manipulator was, the Guild did. Why would they leave Earth without taking it with them?"

"I don't know," said Dad. "Do you, Miss Swervingthorpe?"

"They weren't discussing their plans with me, I assure you."

"They just panicked," said Lady Naomi. "That head guy who was bossing the others around? He was, I think, some sort of unit leader or commander – senior enough to be in charge of this project, but still completely terrified when things were going wrong. He was screaming here about the Guild Mistress – he said she was on her way to inspect the project personally. From what I saw and heard, I imagine as soon as Miss Swervingthorpe escaped into the Nowhere, they were so terrified by their failure they abandoned everything. Probably all just jumped on the first wormhole out of there."

"You mean even Guild members are scared of the Guild?" Amelia asked.

Lady Naomi nodded.

"But wouldn't a device to correctly organize the gateways be kind of a good thing?" said Charlie. "I mean, not in the *Guild's* hands, but –"

"Not in *anyone's* hands," said James bluntly. "No one should have that sort of power."

Charlie looked at him, then nodded slowly. "I get it. Because power corrupts, right?"

"What?" James blinked, and then shook his

head. "No, I don't mean because people can't be trusted with power. I mean because the math predicts total catastrophe. As in: annihilation."

"James is right," said Dad. "We've taken some of his calculations to Control, and they match what they've discovered at every other gateway in the system. The wormholes are in a delicate balance with one another – what happens at one affects every other gateway. If the Guild were able to wrench even one wormhole out of sequence, the injury would ripple through the whole system, magnifying as it went."

Amelia shivered, remembering her brief and violent trip into a wormhole with Krskn and the canister. She remembered the overwhelming power of the gateway, but more than that – she remembered her awareness that the wormhole was somehow *alive*. When Dad talked about the Guild injuring the gateway system, she imagined the wormholes all recoiling, writhing in pain and outrage. Oh, yes, James was right. That could mean annihilation for every connected planet.

"But the wormholes are already out of balance," said Charlie. "There are already blowbacks, the timetables hardly work at all anymore, and the wormholes that *do* bother to turn up are more unstable than ever. How could taming them a bit with this manipulator be any worse?"

"That's just it," said Dad. "Attacking a healthy system would be bad enough, but working against a system that is already chaotic would be sheer lunacy."

"But that's Krskn," Amelia whispered, guts lurching as the truth suddenly hit her.

"What, cookie?"

"Krskn," said Amelia more firmly. "He ... he *planned* it. The whole thing. It was all on purpose. It looked like chaos, but he knew exactly what he was doing the whole time."

"Seriously?" Charlie snorted. "You reckon he

got himself *blown up* and *arrested* on purpose?"

"Yes."

Lady Naomi sucked in a breath. "Amelia's right – I saw him being taken away by Control. He looked ... smug. I thought at the time he was just putting on a show ..."

"But *why?*" said Charlie.

"To get himself taken directly to Control's headquarters," said Amelia. "Why bother trying to discover their location, figure out how to get there, and then how to infiltrate their security –"

"When you can get Control themselves to come and carry you right into the heart of the building," James finished.

"So?" said Charlie. "The canister's gone, isn't it? So what use is the manipulator?"

"It's Krskn," said Lady Naomi bluntly. "I think we can assume he knows exactly where the canister is." She scoffed at herself, disgusted. "All his lies, all his deception and game playing, and once we strip it all away, what's underneath? More lies! A whole other layer to his game! How do I keep falling for it?"

"We all do, Naomi," said Dad. "Not just you. All of Control thought we –"

"Excuse me," said Matilda abruptly. She'd been so quiet, Amelia had almost forgotten her. "Does anyone recognize this phenomenon?"

She pointed to the clearing, and Amelia saw a swirl of green points of light hovering in midair. She'd seen something like it before, and as they watched, the swirl expanded, brightened, and then made a sort of silent "pop" of light, and Tom and Ms. Rosby were standing together, holding the wheel of a teleporter.

Tom's mouth was already open to shout, but when he saw all of them standing there watching him, his voice dried up and his mouth gaped open like a goldfish. His one good eye locked on Matilda.

"Yeah, yeah, Matilda Swervingthorpe, back from the dead," Charlie said dismissively. "Listen, we need to tell you about –"

"No, *you* listen," snapped Tom, finding his voice again. "Krskn –"

"– has just broken out of Gateway Control jail?" Charlie finished.

"By George, old man," Ms. Rosby said, tottering on her cane, "I knew you were good, but this is uncanny. How did you guess the blighter had slipped his leash?"

"Worse than that, I'm afraid," said Dad. "We can guess he stole the Guild artifact from the boardroom, too."

Ms. Rosby squinted at him so hard, her eyes almost disappeared in a riot of wrinkles. Her usually merry face was so fierce, Amelia was nervous.

"I rather think you've been keeping secrets from me, Scott. I won't bother telling you how shabby that is, but I would appreciate you being completely frank with me right now."

"I'm sorry, Metti," Dad rubbed his forehead. "I know I've let you down, only the Keeper –"

"Spare me," Ms. Rosby snapped. "I'm not getting any younger, and Krskn is on the loose. Just tell me why Krskn would risk being shot dead on capture just to get his hands on an object that is of no use to anyone."

Dad looked even more miserable. "It turns out the artifact is a device for manipulating wormholes. With it, the Guild could gain absolute control of the whole gateway system."

"But more likely, they'll just blow us all up," James put in.

"I see. And you kept this from me."

"No!" Dad almost yelped. "We only just found out that part." He pointed at Matilda. "We got some new information from Miss Swervingthorpe just seconds before you arrived."

Ms. Rosby looked at Matilda and nodded in acknowledgement.

"Still," she went on, "I hardly see how this device is any threat. We've had it for decades now, and no one has ever been able to find a single moving part, let alone imagine a use for it."

Dad was so dejected at this point that Lady Naomi spoke for him. "It turns out you were missing a component."

Tom glared at her in warning, but she plowed on with the truth. "There's a power source. The Guild has been after it for a while, and now Krskn has it."

"Or not!" Charlie protested. "It could be lost."

"It's Krskn," said Amelia. "We know it's not lost."

Ms. Rosby regarded them all gravely. "I'm going to assume there is a very good reason – a reason apart from treachery, idiocy, or extreme greed – for why you've kept all this from me."

"The Keeper –" Dad croaked, but Ms. Rosby silenced him with a look.

"I'll *assume* a good reason, and save discussing the facts for later. If, in fact, there *is* a later for any of us. But for now, I need to talk to this Keeper of yours."

"He's unconscious," said Amelia. "He almost killed himself bringing Miss Swervingthorpe back from the Nowhere."

"Right, then. Scott? Miss Swervingthorpe? I'll need you both to come with me instead."

She held out the teleporter to them. Matilda, to Amelia's surprise, looked thrilled. You might have thought that a hundred and forty years in the Nowhere would put her off dematerialization, but apparently not.

"What about us?" said Charlie. "What do we do?"

Ms. Rosby, for the first time ever, looked at Charlie with something less than affection.

"As you always do, Charlie: whatever you want, regardless of what anyone else says."

Dad, as guilty and deflated as a stray dog, gripped onto the teleporter wheel. Lady Naomi gave the green stone back to Matilda, and then, as Matilda grabbed the wheel, there was a reverse swirl of light, and the three of them disappeared.

Tom stood shaking his head in disbelief.

"I had to tell her, Tom," said Lady Naomi. "It's too late for secrets now."

He grunted, neither agreeing with her nor forgiving her.

"Well?" said Charlie. "I still want to know. What do we do?"

"I'll go see to the Keeper," said Tom. "If we've got any mayonnaise in the kitchen, I might be able to speed his recovery. I expect he would have wanted to see that data for himself."

"I made a copy," said Lady Naomi, defensively. "It's all here in my computer."

Tom harrumphed and limped out of the clearing, back to the hotel.

Suddenly, it was just Amelia, Charlie, James and Lady Naomi in her workstation.

"Charlie's right," said Amelia. "There's got to be something we can do."

"Of course there is," Lady Naomi gathered herself. "It turns out, for all of Control's experts, research and equipment, we have Earth's top authority on wormhole manipulation physics right here."

"We do?" Charlie wrinkled his nose.

Lady Naomi turned to James, who flushed in surprise.

"James, do you think you could do the math to work out how Krskn is most likely going to try to deploy the manipulator?"

"Actually, that's pretty easy."

Lady Naomi smiled. "Good. At last something's going our way."

"Yeah ... not quite. The *how* he'll use it is no problem. The *where*, however ..."

"What do you mean?"

"Er, may I?" James indicated Lady Naomi's computer, slightly awkwardly.

"Of course. Here."

Her holo-screen lit up again with an aerial view of Forgotten Bay. It wasn't a map, Amelia knew, but a live satellite feed. Lady Naomi ushered James over to the control panel and he blushed again. He'd been ogling this extraordinary tech for months.

He ummed and ahhed a bit to himself and played with the keyboard. Different-sized circles formed themselves over the image of Forgotten Bay, one inside the other so that they made a bull's-eye, with Tom's cottage and the gateway underneath at the very center.

"What are you doing?" said Charlie.

"*Shh, Charlie!*" said Amelia, who by now knew

much better than to distract a concentrating scientist.

James, though, seemed happy to do his calculations out loud. "Well ... see ... okay: we know the manipulator is untested, so everyone, Krskn included, is going to be working blind here, but ... right! Okay! Look –"

All the circles on the screen disappeared except for a thick orange ring.

"We know from the explosion Krskn triggered last time he opened the canister that it's far too dangerous for him to operate anywhere near the gateway. The inside of this ring is how far the blast extended then."

Amelia shuddered.

"Then," James went on, "if the explosion's force decreased at a fixed rate over distance ... if the canister's maximum capacity ... times pi ... hmm ... and taking air pressure at sea level into account ... yes, I'm sure that the outside of the orange ring is the very closest Krskn could safely deploy his weapon."

Charlie scoffed. "But that means Krskn could be anywhere!"

James shook his head. "Not *any*where." He pressed a button, and a thin band of red appeared around the orange ring. "He needs to be within some kind of range of the gateway and – look, I'll spare you the math, but I'd say he'd be somewhere in the red zone."

Amelia gulped. "And look – half the red zone is over the sea, and the rest is mostly over bushland. But Krskn won't be hiding in the bush – it's better for him to be out in the open."

"Why?"

"It's Control who want to keep aliens secret," Lady Naomi explained. "And it's Control who want to protect humans from the gateway. And from Krskn! So Krskn can turn the town to his advantage. As long as he surrounds himself with innocent people, Control won't be able to attack him."

Charlie paled, then looked at the map again. His face was creased with worry, and then a tiny gleam of hope lit up in him. "But look – the whole town is in the orange zone. Practically the only bit of town land that's in Krskn's zone is the lighthouse headland, and nobody will be there on a weekday."

"Practically," said Amelia. "But not quite. Look here." She pointed to a small bump in the curve of Forgotten Bay. One little jutting lump of land, close to the lighthouse headland, and just inside the red circle.

Charlie stammered in disbelief, his last argument gone. "But that's ..."

Amelia nodded. "That's our school."

CHAPTER FIVE

"Run up to the hotel," said Lady Naomi. "Get your mum to call the school. Tell them –"

"We can't," said Amelia desperately. "The phones are down again. We'll have to go and tell them ourselves."

Exasperation flashed on Lady Naomi's face.

"Tell them *what* exactly?" said James. "No one's going to listen to us."

"Yes, they will," said Lady Naomi, turning to Amelia and Charlie. "Go to Ms. Slaviero. Tell her we've got a Code Black."

"*Ms. Slaviero?*" Charlie squawked. "And – wait.

What's –"

"Just *go*. Trust me. She'll know what it means. James and I will try to come up with something at this end." Lady Naomi rested a hand on each of Amelia's shoulders. "Deliver the warning, and then *get to safety*."

"But –" said Charlie.

"Code Black," Amelia repeated. "Got it."

She grabbed Charlie's arm and dragged him away through the bush.

It was 11 a.m., almost the end of recess, as Amelia and Charlie galloped through town. There were people everywhere: mothers with babies and preschoolers, old folks doing their shopping, people from the city eating ice cream and meat pies in the outdoor cafes. Amelia and Charlie got plenty of odd looks as they pounded along the sidewalk.

Archie, sweeping the step outside his grocery, shouted, "Why aren't you kids in school?"

"On our way," panted Charlie.

Everyone at school was inside, putting away their hats and water bottles, when Amelia and Charlie crashed, red faced and sweaty, through the door to Ms. Slaviero's room.

"Oh, hello," she said mildly, looking up from her desk. "Busy morning for you two, was it? Not enough time to –"

"Code Black!" Charlie practically yelled.

Shani, Dean, Erik and all the rest sniggered to one another, and Amelia saw Sophie F. make a face and twirl her finger by her ear. You didn't have to be a lip-reader to see her whispering, "Cuckoo! Cuckoo!"

But Ms. Slaviero had turned white and was staring at Charlie. "Where did you hear that? What's he playing at, Amelia?"

"It's true, Ms. Slaviero," said Amelia, urgently.

"There's danger coming. If there's something you're meant to do ..." She trailed off, no idea what she was supposed to say or what was supposed to happen next.

Ms. Slaviero nodded, reaching a decision. She pulled her phone from her pocket and hit a number on her speed dial. The other kids looked at Amelia and Charlie, demanding to know what was going on. But Amelia was too busy trying to figure out how in the world Ms. Slaviero knew what a Code Black was.

Whoever was on the other end of Ms. Slaviero's phone call picked up, and she said, "It's Jackie Slaviero. We've got a Code Black ... Yes, I'm sure. Get on with – Okay ... Okay. Yes, that's – Right. Thank you."

She ended the call.

Ms. Slaviero swallowed hard, gathering herself, then clapped her hands together. "Okay. All right, everyone: we're going for a new world record.

Twenty seconds to clear the desks."

There was stunned silence.

"You heard me!" Ms. Slaviero barked. "Just like we do for our disco breaks. Fifteen seconds now – don't pack up your pencils, Ethan! This isn't a drill. Just *move!*"

She stabbed the button on her CD player and "I Will Survive" blasted out at top volume. Confused, but jolted by the music, the kids began clearing the room. Ms. Slaviero opened the connecting door to the next room and called out, "Mr. Whitlock? Code Black – my room in sixty seconds, please."

By the time she pulled her head back, every desk and chair had been shoved against the wall.

"Dean, Erik," she commanded, totally cool now, "grab the corners of the rug. Ethan, Callan, Shani, Taylor – help them pull it back. *Now.* Don't worry about doing it neatly."

The big, stained square of carpet was peeled

back, and underneath, Amelia saw –

"Whoa," said Charlie. "You've got to be kidding."

A shiny steel trapdoor, set into the floor. Ms. Slaviero raced to her desk, felt around underneath it, and pushed a button. With a whir of clockwork, the trapdoor opened, revealing a staircase leading down into the ground.

By now, even with the music blaring, the room seemed quiet. None of the kids had the faintest clue what was happening, but they could feel their teacher's dread and urgency.

Ms. Slaviero switched off the music and smiled stiffly at her class. "Well done, kids. Now, I need you to number off as you head down the stairs. Taylor, you're class monitor this term – will you please go first and switch on the lights as you go? Third step down."

Poor Taylor looked queasy, but she did as she was told.

"One," she called out.

"Two," said Ava, following close behind.

"Three ..."

"Ms. Slaviero," said Callan. "Is it nuclear war?"

"Is it terrorists?" said Sophie F.

The line of kids going into the bunker stalled, waiting for an answer.

Amelia watched her teacher's face flicker.

She doesn't know, Amelia realized. Someone – probably Gateway Control – must have set all this Code Black stuff up in case of emergency. In case something truly disastrous ever came through the gateway. They'd told Ms. Slaviero *what* to do, but they obviously hadn't told her why.

"It's an emergency," said Ms. Slaviero firmly. "It doesn't matter what kind. Right now, I need you all downstairs, safe. And look – here's Mr. Whitlock with the little ones. Don't dawdle! We'll discuss the details once we're all –"

A *thunk* echoed down from the ceiling and all

the lights suddenly switched themselves off.

Someone had cut the power.

Or maybe not *all* the power: seconds later, Amelia heard the ghostly wail of air-raid sirens blaring through Forgotten Bay. She looked at Charlie, eyes wide. Were there secret trapdoors and bunkers all over town?

Ms. Slaviero looked down at the two of them. "When this is all over, I think you and I are going to need to have a talk." Then she turned back to the line of students filing into the trapdoor. "Quickly, Shani."

"My phone's not working! I'm trying to call my mum, but it won't even –"

"It's okay," Ms. Slaviero said smoothly. "We'll call her later." But Amelia saw her sneak a look at her own phone. The screen was dead.

"That's probably what Code Black stands for," Charlie muttered. "Total blackout – they've shut down all communications."

We're alone, Amelia thought. *Control have cut us off from the rest of the world.* She gulped. Was this for their protection? Or were Control so determined to keep the gateway secret from humanity that they'd be willing to abduct a whole town?

"Ms. Slaviero!" said Sophie F., pushing her way back up out of the trapdoor. "Sophie T.'s not down here! You let her run back out to the beach to get her water bottle!"

Ms. Slaviero slapped her forehead. "Mr. Whitlock, will you supervise here? I've got to get Sophie."

She ran out the door, leaving Amelia and Charlie uncertain about what to do next. Mr. Whitlock ushered the last of the little kids down the stairs, then poked his head back out of the bunker.

"Come on, please, Charlie. Amelia." He waved them over.

Amelia looked out the door for Ms. Slaviero,

stalling. Lady Naomi had told them to get to safety – but were they seriously just going to hide out in a bunker with Krskn on the loose and their families still out there?

"Now!" snapped Mr. Whitlock. "It's Code Black! No exceptions, no questions, we follow procedure. Now get down here, Mr. Floros."

"Yeesh, brainwashed much?" Charlie said under his breath to Amelia. "I say we run for it."

"Charlie!" Mr. Whitlock commanded. "Now. You too, Amelia."

"It's okay," said Ms. Slaviero, jogging back through the doorway. "They were just waiting for me."

Mr. Whitlock nodded. "Fine, fine. Let's just get down there. We should have the bunker sealed from inside within ten minutes of the alarm."

"But what about Sophie T.?" asked Charlie.

Ms. Slaviero frowned. "What about her?"

"Where is she?"

"Sophie T. is fine," said Ms. Slaviero. "Perfectly safe. Right now, you children need to get down into the bunker with all your friends."

"But we can't just ..." Amelia's breath caught in her throat, cutting the sentence short.

Suspicion sparked through her.

No. It wasn't possible ...

"Oh, *honestly*," Ms. Slaviero sighed heavily, confirming Amelia's worst fears. "Why do you two always have to make everything so *difficult?*"

She reached behind her as though to scratch her shoulder blade, and when she brought her hand back it was holding a sleek, black, and definitely *alien* pistol, which she trained on Amelia and Charlie.

Mr. Whitlock gasped, "Jackie! What are you doing?"

"I'm doing what no one else in forty-nine galaxies has ever been able to do," she grinned brilliantly, and put her hand up to her neck. "I'm winning *everything.*"

She dug her fingers into the flesh of her throat, pulled out a tiny black-and-brass holo-emitter and tossed it to Amelia.

Ms. Slaviero flickered and disappeared. In her place stood an equally familiar but much less welcome figure – dark, sinuous, ridiculously beautiful, gloating as he lashed his tail.

Krskn.

CHAPTER SIX

"Great," Charlie murmured in Amelia's ear, as screams filtered up from the bunker stairwell behind them. "So much for secrecy."

"Told you," Amelia hissed back. "He's going to do it all out in the open."

Krskn grinned at the sounds of terror reverberating around the classroom. He held up a hand. "Thank you, thank you – my theme song, right there. Ah, it warms my heart to hear it. All right, that's enough now. Shush."

He paced toward them. Amelia and Charlie held their ground uncertainly, standing between Krskn and the bunker.

How long had Krskn been here? And what had happened to the *real* Ms. Slaviero?

It couldn't have been Krskn the whole time, or he wouldn't have called in the Code Black. He must have attacked Ms. Slaviero and taken her place when she went out to find Sophie T. Which meant that now *two* people Amelia cared about were missing.

As Krskn came closer, Amelia saw that something bizarre had happened to him: strange horns were protruding from his back. Then she understood – it was the manipulator. Of course. Black against black, it had blended into his matte salamander skin, becoming almost part of his body.

It suits him, she thought. *Beautiful, cruel and insanely dangerous.* The Guild had picked their operative well.

Amelia shook herself. This was no time to be dazzled by the creep. She had to try to shift the balance. Because if Krskn was the guy the Guild chose as their representative, what in the world must the rest of them be like? They couldn't afford to find out.

"So, Krksn," she said, and was pleased to hear her voice sounding almost as unimpressed as Charlie's usually was. "What's the big plan? I know you love proving how tough you are by scaring little kids, but –"

"Scaring little kids?" Krskn narrowed his red eyes and smirked, pulling the manipulator off his back with his free hand and pointing it at her, along with the first weapon. "Oh no, Amelia, I adore children. They're so endlessly gullible, so weirdly precious to adults, and such easily transportable little hostages."

Amelia shivered. No way was she going to let Krskn kidnap her – or any of her friends – ever again.

"Now," Krskn continued, yawning hugely,

"step aside, both of you. I need them all out of the bunker."

"Look here, sir," said Mr. Whitlock behind them, standing on the stairs between the kids below and Krskn. "If you need a hostage, take me, but –"

He fell silent at a venomous glare from Krskn.

"Out of the bunker," Krskn repeated, and waggled the manipulator meaningfully.

"Or what?" said Charlie. "I mean, yeah, sweet weapon, Krskn. But we both know it's useless without the canister."

"*This* one isn't," Krskn reminded him, twitching the little black pistol in his other hand.

Charlie faltered for a moment. "True," he said, a little shakier than before. "But you didn't come halfway across the universe and get yourself arrested for *that* one. So until you can find the canister – which is totally lost, by the way – this is all pointless."

Krskn sighed. "My dear imbecile, do you honestly think I've let go of that canister for even a heartbeat? It's been with me ever since I first touched it."

"Ha," said Charlie. "I call your bluff."

But he flicked an uneasy look at Amelia. Deceptive, treacherous, and evil as he was, Krskn was also oddly honest in his boasts.

And indeed, Krskn's smile widened, showing off all his teeth to the very last molar, and then, in sickening slow motion, they watched as his lower jaw distended, dislocated and sagged loosely against his throat. His mouth was now an obscene, gaping maw. His whole body shuddered, beginning with the very tip of his tail, then building in intensity up his belly until his long neck was wracked by spasms.

"Any hope he's choking to death?" asked Charlie, repulsed.

For a flickering moment, Amelia wondered if

they should seize the opportunity to make a run at him. But instead she just looked on, mesmerized, as Krskn slid his gun into a holster on his thigh, and used his free hand to reach down inside his own mouth. His hand sank deep into his gullet, so far that half his forearm followed, and Amelia began gagging in helpless sympathy. Behind her, she heard one of the kids in the bunker let out a shriek of revulsion.

With a horrible slurping sound, Krskn drew back his arm. And there, clenched in his fist, dripping with thick ropes of saliva, was the canister.

Charlie gasped, jabbing an elbow into Amelia's side, like he was trying to get her attention.

Yeah, thought Amelia. *Don't worry – I'm watching.*

Then she realized it wasn't Krskn that Charlie had been gasping at.

Sophie T. had just snuck into the classroom

89

through Mr. Whitlock's connecting door.

She was holding a cricket bat.

Krskn's jaw slid back up into place, and after a couple of experimental champs at the air, he licked his lips and grinned at his audience.

"I don't suppose you know much about Hykryk physiology," Krskn said, sliding the canister into the manipulator. Instantly, dozens of tiny orange lights sparked up along the black curves. "We swallow our eggs, and let the young hatch inside us. Vomit them up once they're ready for the outside world. But better than that, by some happy fluke, our gestation sacs are practically impervious to any scanning technology in the universe."

Behind him, Sophie T. took another terrified step forward.

"Well," he corrected himself. "We're impervious to any of *Control's* scanning technology. Naturally, the Guild are superior in this, as they are in every other field. You'll see that once they've conquered your world and put you all in service to the glorious Guild Mistress."

Amelia stared determinedly at Krskn, trying not to give Sophie T. away with her eyes. Her heart was beating so hard, she thought her rib cage was about to explode. Sophie T. was halfway between the doorway and Krskn now, totally exposed. If Krskn turned his head only a degree or two more, he'd see her.

"You know," Charlie said loudly. "You're really not the kind of guy I imagined being so excited to be someone else's servant."

Krskn blinked. "A servant?" he hissed. "Is that really what you see when you look at me?"

Charlie shrugged. "You're the one who just said how awesome it was going to be to serve your Guild Mistress. It sounded like you were talking from experience."

Krskn hissed again, baring his teeth, and

Amelia cringed as snakelike fangs slid out of his gums.

Charlie, she silently pleaded with him. *Be careful!*

Krskn took a step closer, his tail lashing. Sophie T. had to skip backward to avoid being hit. She grimaced and gripped the bat more tightly, raising it high over her head and waiting for her chance. She was so white with fear, her blond hair looked dark against her skin.

"Let me see," Krskn said, icily quiet, lisping slightly through his fangs. "One of us is holding a device that will utterly restructure the universe – a device that he recaptured all by himself with nothing but his own genius. The other is a very small and grubby human larva that is about to be shot. Which one of us do you think is more like a –"

Krskn's eyes bulged from his head as Sophie T. brought the cricket bat down with all her strength on his tail. The gills stood out on his neck, and his whole body froze in agony. Before he could move, Sophie T. struck again, and then again – all her disgust and fear of aliens being channeled into a murderous attack on that tail.

Amelia, seizing her chance, grabbed one of the chairs from behind her. She yelled at Mr. Whitlock, who was still standing halfway up the bunker stairs, "Get down – *now!*"

She swung the chair and hit Krskn square in the face, while Charlie darted forward and pulled the gun from Krskn's numb hand. He leaped back again, training the pistol on Krskn.

Krskn lifted the manipulator and pointed it back at Charlie.

Amelia dived for Ms. Slaviero's desk. She fumbled blindly, found the button hidden underneath it, and mashed it with her palm. With a whir of clockwork, the trapdoor in the floor slid shut, sealing Mr. Whitlock and the rest of the students safely inside.

A scream rebounded off the walls, and Amelia leaped up again, just in time to see Krskn's arm clamp down around Sophie T.'s throat. He pulled her tight against his chest, still aiming the manipulator at Charlie with his other hand. The tiny orange lights on the device had deepened to a bloody red.

Charlie kept the tiny black pistol pointed at Krskn, but it was an almost empty gesture.

Krskn snarled at them, his breath ragged.

"Outside," he said. "You've got work to do."

CHAPTER SEVEN

"Move," Krskn ordered.

They shuffled awkwardly toward the door. Charlie kept the stolen pistol pointed at Krskn, but Amelia knew there was no way he'd fire it while Krskn had Sophie T. clutched to his chest.

Krskn, for his part, pointed the manipulator right back at Charlie as he dragged Sophie T. out into the playground after them. With a jerk of his head, he directed them all down to the beach.

They were edging their way out of the school grounds and up the narrow path over the dunes, the soft sand making it hard to walk backward, when Amelia stepped on something solid. She yelped and skipped sideways when she realized she'd trodden on Ms. Slaviero's wrist.

Amelia dropped to her knees beside her teacher. Ms. Slaviero was out cold, sprawled on her back in the sand with an ugly purple bruise in the middle of her forehead. She was still breathing, but –

"Leave her," snapped Krskn. "Worry about yourself, while you still can. Or worry about your friend here, if you prefer."

Sophie T., still half-choked by Krskn's arm across her throat, narrowed her eyes. As scared as she was, she was furious with Krskn.

They made their way across the beach, splashed across the storm water creek, and went up past the shark carcass to the very foot of the lighthouse headland.

"All right, my poppet," said Krskn, loosening his hold on Sophie T. but fixing her in one spot with a clawed hand on her shoulder. He stared into her eyes, his own huge, red eyes unblinking. "I'm trusting you to stand here when I let you go. I trust you to be sensible, and not try to run away because I can tell you're much smarter than your friends here. Smart enough to know you wouldn't make it two steps. You are that smart, aren't you?"

Sophie T. nodded, dazed. Amelia well knew how hypnotic those red eyes could be.

"Right." Krskn had stationed Sophie T. between himself and Charlie. Looking for a way to distract Krskn, Amelia stepped away to the side, out of the line of fire – but so what? What was she going to do, kick sand at him?

Krskn stroked the curl of lights along the manipulator, and then pressed several of them in a complicated sequence. Three thin legs dropped from the device, and Krskn planted the tripod in the sand. He directed the largest end of the manipulator out across the water, aiming it for the other headland – the *gateway* headland. *It was the perfect position,* Amelia realized. Where the manipulator stood, there was a relatively short stretch of beach, and then nothing but the sea between it and the other headland. The whole curve of Forgotten Bay – the town, the beach, and all the people – was off to one side, like the audience in a play.

To get to the manipulator, you'd have to get past Krskn – unless some rescue could come to them out of the water? Amelia didn't think that was likely. So Krskn had the whole ocean protecting him on one side, and the whole town between him and Control on the other. And the manipulator had a clear shot toward the gateway in between. And the only people around to stop him were Charlie (unable to shoot because of Sophie T.) and Amelia.

"You have spoiled today's field trip for your class, Amelia," Krskn said, as though he knew what she was thinking. He pressed the tiny lights on the manipulator again. This time, there was a deep, throbbing sound, and the lights turned blue and started flickering. "I wanted your whole school here. What I'm doing is extraordinary – the first time anything of this magnitude or magnificence has been attempted anywhere in the universe. And you've selfishly left all your friends locked underground like a coward!" He sighed. "All this glory and power, and just three of you here with me to see it."

The manipulator throbbed more loudly, the lights flickering with mesmerizing speed, and Amelia glanced hopelessly at Charlie. Krskn's smile widened –

And then he flinched, his eyes fixing on something over Amelia's shoulder.

"Right – as if we're falling for that," said Charlie.

But Sophie T. was staring now, too.

Amelia turned, and saw a figure crossing the sand toward them.

"Ugh, what is *that?*" said Charlie, finally twisting his head to look.

The alien was tall – taller probably than James – but so lumpy and misshapen it looked squat. Its skin was a murky gray-green, and as pebbly, knobbly and slimy looking as a sea squirt. It didn't have what Amelia could recognize as a head. It walked upright on two legs, and had arms (four of them, each with two elbows); its mouths (three) and eyes (half a dozen or so) were embedded in its torso.

Without a doubt, it was the most grotesque thing Amelia had ever seen (and given that they'd just watched Krskn reach down inside his own gut, that was really saying something). Yet the fluttering robes that wafted behind it were gorgeous and gauzy, the bracelets up its arms were clearly worth a fortune, and it strode across the sand with stately dignity.

Krskn took a backward step. "Guild Mistress!"

"Krskn." The voice was phlegmy and cold.

"Oh, your eminence," Krskn bowed deeply. "What, if I dare to ask, are you doing here?"

"Are you questioning me, lowest of underlings?"

"Never, your radiance!" Amelia was shocked to see Krskn cringe. His eyes were lowered, his neck stooped. "I am merely wondering why I should be so favored as to have you here on this squalid planet to see my most humble efforts for the Guild."

Charlie – too shocked to point the gun anywhere – made a face.

"Your humble efforts can go to the sewers, where they belong," the Guild Mistress said calmly. "I am here for my prize. I trust you haven't forgotten that the treasure you hold in your hand belongs to me? That it is, in fact, a perversion of all rank and decency for it to be touched by you at all?"

"Your sublimity!" Krskn bowed lower, but

Amelia saw his eyes flash for the smallest of instants. "Had I even the first inklings of a clue of the possibility that you yourself might deign ..."

Amelia was distracted from Krskn's torrent of apology by Sophie T., standing sideways between the two of them, waggling her fingers. Not daring to move from the spot Krskn had plonked her, too frightened to even turn her head in case it caught his attention, Sophie T. was frantically gesturing with the hand hidden from him.

Amelia kept her face expressionless, but cast her eyes around. At first she saw nothing. Then a glint of sunlight reflected off something, and was gone again. She squinted, and realized that behind the dunes, someone was hiding, watching. She lifted her gaze and saw camouflaged figures creeping into position on the lighthouse headland.

She glanced at Sophie T., who looked meaningfully past Amelia and Charlie. Amelia guessed there must be more people behind her –

perhaps even enough to encircle them completely.

Guild? Amelia gulped, and then decided, *No, surely the Guild would show themselves plainly. They'd all be lining up behind their mistress like a parade.*

So then ... could it be Control?

She blinked. There was more going on than she'd guessed.

Maybe this is part of the Code Black?

Krskn was still groveling, but the Guild Mistress had had enough of him and waved one of her hands. "Silence. Your words are nothing to me. Only your obedience has any value."

"Of course, your splendor."

"Shut down the manipulator."

Krskn stood upright and looked at the throbbing, blazing device. Those flickering lights had paled and brightened to a piercing violet.

"It's too late," he said simply, and looked towards the Guild Mistress in puzzlement. "You can see that –"

"Impudent wretch! I'll say when it's too late."
Krskn bared his teeth, sneering.

"Ah, that single step too far," he laughed. "You almost had me."

The Guild Mistress said nothing, and Charlie raised his weapon again, not sure where to point it yet, but aware the game had shifted.

"I'm assuming it's you, Keeper," Krskn grinned. "Control wouldn't know the Guild Mistress if their lives depended on it. Which they do, by the way."

The Guild Mistress reached up a hand to the top of her lumpen body and pushed her fingers under the flesh above one eye, manipulating a holo-emitter. The awful creature flickered and, a moment later, Leaf Man stood in front of them all, in his usual human guise. Given that he was always painfully thin and impossibly pale, it was hard to say he looked more sickly than usual, but Amelia thought he seemed fragile.

Of course he is, Amelia realized. Even if he hadn't just worn himself out retrieving Matilda Swervingthorpe from the Nowhere, the canister was open, its power flowing through the manipulator – it must have been poisoning him every second he stood there!

Sophie T. cried out as Krskn grabbed hold of her again, yanking her to him. He laughed, lifted his chin, and called out around them with a ringing, bold voice, "Come on – out you come, Control! Don't be shy. This is a great day for the entire universe, and you – worthless, defeated traitors though you are – are nevertheless getting front-row seats. Roll up! Roll up! Let's see who's here!"

After a moment's hesitation, Control agents began to emerge from behind every rock, bush, sand dune and park bench around them. Amelia turned at last to look behind her, and saw her own parents, James, Tom, Lady Naomi, and Charlie's mum, Mary. Even tiny Ms. Rosby was holding onto Dad's arm as they crossed the sand.

"Yes," said Krskn with an approving nod, as the manipulator began to groan. "That's more like it. A real audience!" Then, all at once, the manipulator's dozens of tiny lights blinked off, and Krskn crowed, "It's done! Stand back and watch the new world begin!"

Intense violet light now radiated from every curl of the manipulator, building into a ball of fiery plasma as tall as Krskn. The noise was harrowing, shaking Amelia down to her bones, and nightmarishly familiar. It was the same rushing power as the gateway, only here, instead of wild and joyous, it sounded twisted. Pained.

Whatever the manipulator was going to do, however it worked, Amelia knew it was somehow torturing the gateway.

"Stop it!" she screamed. She clapped her hands over her ears. "It's cruel! You're killing it!"

But it was too late. As Leaf Man fell to the ground, a beam of light shot from the center of the plasma ball, beaming low across the sand, skimming across the bay, and blasting into the base of the hotel's headland.

CHAPTER EIGHT

Huge chunks of rock exploded from the gateway cliff face, landing in the sea with splashes larger than even the crashing waves, visible across the whole expanse of the bay. The beam pounded into the rock, drilling into the headland in a riot of noise. And then –

Amelia's eyes narrowed on another dark shape falling into the water below. Though it happened too fast for her to really see, she could've sworn that this object had fallen from the *top* of the cliff. Her heart skipped a beat, but she saw nothing bob up on the surface.

And still the violet beam thundered into the headland. It was angled so that, though the light was only about waist high at their end, by the time it reached the opposite side of the bay, it was hitting the cliffs several feet above sea level. Amelia could only assume that it made a direct line to the caves under Tom's cottage. That the manipulator was aiming for the very heart of the gateway.

"Cookie!" Dad yelled, drawing her attention away again. "Come here! Charlie – you too!"

Amelia ignored him. Even if she *could* move fast enough to get away from Krskn, it was far too late to worry about safety now. This manipulator was about to change the whole universe – where exactly did Dad think she could go to get away from it?

"You know," Krskn mused, "I wish the Guild Mistress were here. Not that I won't be *richly* rewarded when I present this device to her, but it seems a shame for her not to witness the greatest triumph of my –"

He broke off as Sophie T., still gripped tightly against his chest, gave a sudden, violent jerk. She slipped out of his grasp, darting behind him before he had time to recover. Without a second's pause, she drove her foot, heel down, onto his tail.

Krskn howled with pain, reeling back, and Sophie T. stumbled away, sprinting over to Dad and Ms. Rosby.

The instant she was clear, a couple of trigger-happy Control agents opened fire. Robbed of his human shield, Krskn dived to the sand, narrowly avoiding the blasts of their weapons.

"Hold your fire!" Mum bellowed.

Charlie swung the pistol around to the place where Krskn had hit the sand – but he was already gone.

Amelia wheeled in a circle. *Where* –

Her question was answered almost instantly as Krskn leaped back out from behind the enormous glowing sphere. He shot across the sand, snatching his weapon back from Charlie, and then lunged at Amelia, dragging her up against his chest in place of Sophie T.

"Together again, little bridesmaid," Krskn murmured in her ear. "And look – here comes the bride!"

Amelia, eyes watering as she tried to get a breath, saw Lady Naomi glaring.

"Charlie!" shrieked Mary. "Get over here now!"

Charlie stayed where he was and put his hands on his hips. "Now what, Krskn? You blow up the whole gateway system, and then what happens? You're totally surrounded. Even if you shoot a couple of us, there are enough weapons pointed at you right now to kill you twenty times over."

"I'm not going to *die*, you ridiculous child." Krksn pointed at the manipulator. "Don't you understand what that thing is doing? You can surround me with a thousand Control guns, and I'll still walk past you all. In just a moment or two, this light path will connect with the gateway, and form my own personal wormhole to MN-5."

Amelia flinched. MN-5 was a major Guild stronghold – maybe *the* major Guild stronghold. From what she could gather, it was at the center of their whole return to power. If a wormhole to MN-5 suddenly connected here in the middle of the beach ...

"That's right," said Krskn, feeling Amelia jolt. "Whether you kill me or not, I'm afraid your time is *already* up. The Guild are on their way. This process is unstoppable, irreversible, and an army stands ready to crush this planet into dust."

The sphere of light pulsed, and somewhere inside it, the manipulator shuddered and whined. The ground under Amelia's feet vibrated. She looked around at the circle of Control agents –

and saw other figures, farther off, moving in to join them.

Humans, she realized with dismay.

So much for the Code Black. Whatever rules the residents of Forgotten Bay were supposed to be following, it seemed as though a sizeable number of them were courageous enough or curious enough or just plain *dumb* enough to have come to see what was happening.

Control would be furious. Right now, though, keeping Control's secrets was the least of Amelia's worries.

The beam of violet light was thickening, writhing slightly, and hanging bizarrely in the air.

"Look – it's almost through," said Krskn happily, gazing at the cliff face across the bay. Indeed, rock had stopped falling in such huge slabs, and the beam of light seemed to be deep inside the headland. It couldn't be long now until it hit the underground chamber of the gateway.

Forget this, Amelia thought. She wasn't about to spend her last moments on Earth being Krskn's puppet. She needed to find a way to get free of Krskn and clear the way for the Control guys to come and grab him.

There was no way she could run away without him shooting her, but if she could do what Sophie T. had done – if she could drop to the ground fast enough, and if the Control guys reacted fast enough, she might be able to give one of them a clear shot. It wasn't exactly a plan – but it was their only chance to gain the advantage.

Without warning, Amelia jerked all her weight downward, shifting in Krskn's grip. But even as her chest and face escaped his arm, his tail flicked up and smacked her across the stomach, knocking the wind out of her. She kept struggling.

"Enough!" he commanded, but Amelia wasn't stopping for anything. And thanks to Sophie T., she now knew Krskn's weak spot. She lunged forward, wrapped both arms around his tail and bit him as hard as she could. Krskn let out a scream, and Amelia found herself sprawling to the ground on her hands and knees.

A foot – Krskn's – came down on Amelia's back, pinning her to the sand. She heard shouts, gasps, the roar and groan of the manipulator – and then a massive blast exploded in her ears, and for a moment, Amelia couldn't hear anything.

Krskn had pulled the trigger on his pistol.

The ringing in Amelia's ears dissipated, replaced by more gasps and screams – and this time, Tom's hoarse cry rang out above them all: "You shot her!"

"No – I'm okay," she wanted to reassure him, but she couldn't speak. It was all she could do to lift her head and look over at them all, hoping her family would see her face and know she was still alive. But what she saw made her wish she'd been shot after all.

All at once, she saw exactly what her escape attempt had achieved – what it had cost.

Tom, his mouth open in an endless, silent cry, was staring at Lady Naomi.

Lady Naomi stood, very still, halfway between Amelia's family and Krskn, her angular gray eyes wide, her tawny skin suddenly grayish, and both her hands pressed against her stomach.

For a long, long moment, nothing moved. Nothing happened. Nothing but the throb and hum of the manipulator. And then bright drops of blood began spilling out from between Lady Naomi's fingers. Her mouth made an *O* shape, and she pitched forward, collapsing into the sand.

CHAPTER NINE

Tom let out a wail of anguish and ran to Lady Naomi's side, crashing to his knees in the sand.

"There," said Krskn, his foot still pinning Amelia down, "do you see what happens when you won't do as you're told?"

Krskn reached down, hauling Amelia up in front of him again. She was too horrified to even fight him.

What have I done?

She'd thought she was helping, and now ...

The ground heaved beneath them, and the light from the manipulator to the gateway seemed to intensify. The almost-solid beam of violet light was strengthened and deepened by a matching beam of light coming back the other way. The connection with the gateway had been made.

"Ah, something's working anyway," said Krskn. "Look, Amelia – you've cost me my wife, but you get to see the first engineered wormhole connect to MN-5. Aren't you lucky?"

Threads of green and purple began to shoot through the beam, and then channels of that impossible color Amelia remembered from her trip inside the gateway.

It's over. Everything's over.

A roar of desperate energy exploded inside Amelia, and she let out a howl of fury, kicking and fighting under Krskn's grip. Krskn tightened his hold on her –

And then staggered in shock, his attention turning to Lady Naomi again.

Amelia stopped struggling.

Her mouth dropped open.

Lady Naomi was getting to her feet.

The hair on the back of Amelia's neck prickled. When Krskn had opened the canister back in the caves, Lady Naomi had surged with sudden strength, as though the substance inside it had the opposite effect on her than Leaf Man.

Could it be enough to save her? If Control could get to her fast enough with whatever aliens used for first aid ...

"My darling!" Krskn crowed. "You are an utter marvel! You never cease to amaze me. But don't come any closer, lover, or I'll shoot you again. And on purpose this time, so you know it will count."

Lady Naomi's mouth was set in an angry line, both hands still pressed against her stomach, and her shirt was dark with blood. She staggered a bit as she stood, but she shook off Tom's attempt to help her, and kept her eyes fixed on Krskn. She was so ashen, Amelia expected her to collapse again, but Lady Naomi forced herself to walk.

"Oh, sweetheart," Krskn chided. "Don't doubt me. Don't come any closer."

But Amelia realized Lady Naomi wasn't. At first it had looked as though Lady Naomi were faltering, weaving because of the pain. In truth, though, Lady Naomi was deliberately heading *sideways* – not towards Krskn at all.

She was heading for the beam blasting out from the manipulator. And with each step she took, she stood a little straighter, her eyes a little more fierce.

"Naomi!" Tom called.

Amelia knew that the pulsing energy flow was somehow recharging Lady Naomi, perhaps working like a kind of anesthetic, but Amelia seconded Tom's worry. Being around the canister's contents was one thing; getting too close to the raw substance itself was quite another. Surely the manipulator's beam was too dangerous even for Lady Naomi.

"My darling ..." said Krskn, still pointing his gun at her. He took his foot off Amelia's back and stepped toward Lady Naomi. "What are you –"

"Now!" shouted Charlie, and he, James and Dad all threw themselves at Krskn, knocking him to the ground in a flying rugby tackle.

"The gun, James!" yelled Dad. "Get the gun!"

Charlie grunted as Krskn kicked him viciously in the stomach, but clung on. Amelia rolled out of the way, too winded and sore to help.

Mum was beside Amelia in a flash, scooping her up into her arms, and she heard Ms. Rosby yell to her agents, "Secure Krskn! I want him totally immobilized before this wormhole is functional!"

The manipulator kept throbbing, and the throb was joined now by a deep crackling sound – like a peal of thunder that went on and on. Amelia squirmed around in Mum's embrace to see Lady Naomi reach her hand *into* the beam. Threads of light reached out from the beam to Lady Naomi, and wound themselves around her fingers and wrist.

"Wait! Stop!" Tom and Krskn cried out together.

Lady Naomi, her shirt drenched in blood, ignored them both. She looked strangely separate from the world, as though she knew she were already dead, but didn't care one bit. Her face, still haggard from the pain and blood loss, was also weirdly excited. She stared at the tendrils of light swarming up her arm, and she smiled.

"Oh my word," Mum murmured, holding onto Amelia. "She's hypnotized by it – she's like a moth to a flame."

More like a bug zapper, thought Amelia, wincing as another crackling feather of light broke off from the main beam and traced its way up the twisted silver scar that ran from Lady Naomi's wrist to

her shoulder. Her whole arm was engulfed.

And then, with a sudden leap, Lady Naomi plunged her whole body into the beam.

Krskn froze, and Dad, James and Charlie, all pinning him down, froze too, their struggle forgotten as they stared.

For a moment, Lady Naomi simply stood there, and the beam blasted straight through the middle of her so that she was like a bead on a string. And then, so quickly it happened between one eye blink and the next, the light swarmed over her, absorbing her as it had absorbed her arm.

Amelia cried out. It was horrible – Lady Naomi had gone, melted away into the wormhole's energy. There was nothing left of her but a thicker blob in the beam.

The light grew brighter, and as it did, so did Amelia's sense that the wormhole was in pain. Perhaps Lady Naomi's pain was adding to it.

Whatever the case, the light was now too strong to look at, the noise too deafening to bear. Just before Amelia turned her face away, she saw the blob that had been Lady Naomi begin to slide along the beam toward the manipulator. That impossible gateway color was sparkling and swirling chaotically in the blob, but Amelia couldn't look any longer. She hid against Mum's chest, her hands over her ears, and Mum wrapped her arms around her.

The noise kept building until it was an inhuman scream of rage and torment, and then there was a burst of light so terrible that Amelia could see it even with her eyes shut, and her face pressed against Mum.

And then nothing.

At first, Amelia's ears were ringing so badly, she didn't know the noise had stopped. Then, when she opened her eyes, it was hard to focus on anything. Not only was the midday sun so pale and watery by comparison that it felt like twilight, but whatever Amelia looked at was confused by flickering afterimages on her retinas.

But she felt the sand under her feet, so the Earth must still be there. And gradually, other noises came back to her ears. First, the pound of the surf on the beach, then cries of alarm and outrage.

"He's getting away!" James yelled.

Amelia made out a lithe black shape speeding across the sand toward the water. Gunshots popped and whizzed from the semicircle of Control agents, but Krskn was too fast and too far away for accuracy. With a tiny splash, he dove under the water and disappeared.

"Now what?" yelled Charlie. "How do we get him now?"

Amelia, though, couldn't care less about Krskn. She was gazing, baffled, at another figure.

The sand where the manipulator had stood

was now fused into a shallow bowl of dirty glass. In the bottom of it was a smoldering pile of ash. The remains, Amelia guessed, of the manipulator. And standing in the ash, very still and faintly glowing, was Lady Naomi.

Tom got to her first, limping so fast he almost tripped over. But just as he arrived at the edge of the bowl, he stopped. Too shy, perhaps, to touch her, or even to speak to her.

He was still standing dumbfounded when Amelia and Mum reached him. They stood together, wondering, and then Lady Naomi turned and saw them looking at her, and smiled. Not her usual self-conscious smile, but a delighted grin.

"Did you see that?" she laughed, amazed.

Amelia heard herself laughing back. Lady Naomi? Alive? It was impossible, ridiculous, and almost beyond belief, even with Lady Naomi standing right there in front of her.

Ever since they'd arrived in Forgotten Bay,

the gateway had been getting more and more dangerous, and the consequences had been more and more severe. How could it be that when the very worst moment came, when everything went wrong, when all hope was gone and the end of the world was certain, what they got instead was this?

"Did we see it?" Amelia repeated. "It was pretty hard to miss."

She looked up at the headland and bay and realized just how many people were there. More and more people from the town had come out to watch, and coming over the sand dunes was the rest of Forgotten Bay Primary. And there was Ms. Slaviero with them, recovered from Krskn's assault. Faint cheers carried on the sea breeze.

"Oh," said Amelia, looking at Mum in alarm. "*Everyone* saw it, didn't they?"

"What," Charlie panted, dashing over to them, "was that?"

Sophie T., Mary and Ms. Rosby came over too. If Sophie T. had been starstruck by Lady Naomi before, now she looked almost worshipful.

Lady Naomi laughed again. "I don't know, but wasn't it great?"

"But how did you do it?" Charlie insisted. "How did you stop the Guild getting through?"

"Did I?" Lady Naomi looked puzzled. "Was that me?"

"Well, no one else was crazy enough to jump into the beam."

Lady Naomi grinned again. "I don't know. I really don't understand what happened, I just ... knew."

"Knew what?" said Amelia.

"I don't know! Or I can't remember now. It seemed very clear and obvious at the time, but now it feels like a dream. All the details are falling away."

"But," Tom croaked, "what about your stomach?"

"Hmm?" Lady Naomi smiled at him. "Oh, the

gunshot wound. I forgot all about that, too." She pulled up the hem of her ruined T-shirt and revealed a flat, tawny expanse of unmarked stomach. There was no blood, not even a mark where the blast had hit her.

"And your arm," said Sophie T. in a hushed voice. "Look!"

Lady Naomi looked at one arm and then the other, bemused, but Amelia knew what Sophie T. meant.

"Your scar is gone!"

"Oh, yes!"

Both of Lady Naomi's arms were now equally smooth; the awful snake of silvery scar tissue had vanished as if it had never been there.

"Fascinating!" said Ms. Rosby.

There were roars of alarm from the shoreline, then James yelled, "No, don't shoot! Wait!" and they all turned to see what new trouble was upon them.

Amelia laughed. Not trouble; it was Grawk, dog-paddling through the surf, riding on the crest of a wave, making his way to the beach with something in his mouth.

"Oh, wow," said Sophie T. faintly. "Has he gotten bigger again?"

"Hold your fire!" Dad bellowed, and to Amelia's relief, Arxish, one of the top three Control agents along with Ms. Rosby, backed up the command.

Grawk padded from the water, dragging a limp, black, rag-like thing with him.

"Oh, it's Krskn!" Amelia clapped her hands. "Grawk's got him by the tail."

"Well, go on," Arxish bawled at his agents. "What are you waiting for? Someone go and arrest that maniac."

The agents looked less than enthusiastic. Arresting Krskn was daunting enough, but taking him from the jaws of this enormous monster?

"Excuse me," Amelia said joyfully, and ran

down to see her friend. "Grawk! You hero! I saw you diving from the cliff."

Grawk gave Krskn a hard shake, dropped him in the sand at the feet of a dozen agents, and then bounded over to Amelia.

She heard distant screams of shock as the huge beast charged at her, and for a split second she was nervous herself. Sharp white teeth flashed past her face, and then she was on her back in the sand and he was nuzzling her belly and making her squirm with laughter, tickling her mercilessly the way she'd tickled him when he was a puppy.

"Oh, stop! Stop it, Grawk," she begged, laughing. "Oh, you've got shark breath – it's horrible! Stop!"

"Hey, Grawk," said Charlie. "You'd really better stop – everyone thinks you're eating her alive."

Grawk sat back in the sand and wagged his tail.

"*Grawk!*" he barked, and as Amelia stood up, he gave her one last almighty lick with his massive purple tongue.

She brushed the sand off herself, still laughing, and then looked around at the scores of human faces staring at her and Grawk, or at Lady Naomi like a phoenix in her glass dish, or at Krskn being hauled up the beach by Control agents with their distinctly alien weaponry. People were pointing at the gaping hole in the gateway headland, and everywhere there was the sound of urgent discussion.

Charlie smiled. "I can't wait to see how they cover this one up."

CHAPTER TEN

Ms. Slaviero looked a bit shaky on her feet as she made her way toward Amelia and Charlie. Mr. Whitlock was hovering at her elbow, and behind them, a mob of school kids followed. Some of the kids looked excited, some were more on the terrified-out-of-their-minds side of the spectrum. And a lot were simply bewildered, waiting for Ms. Slaviero to explain it all to them just like she always did.

"Well, you got me there, kids," she called, holding her forehead with one hand. "I thought

I was prepared for anything, but that was ... something else."

"Sorry Krskn got you," said Amelia.

"Is that the scrawny lizard fellow?"

"Yeah."

"Hmm. At first I thought he was a bit of a spunk, but being pistol-whipped quickly changed my mind." She smiled and nodded appreciatively to Grawk. "Thank you for being so rough with him just then."

"Oh, this is Grawk," said Amelia. "Grawk, this is Ms. Slaviero. But he doesn't talk," she added quickly.

"*Grawk!*" he barked.

"Well, all right, you can say *grawk*, but that's not what I meant."

Ms. Slaviero regarded them. "I don't suppose either of you would like to tell me what all this was about?"

"Er ..." Amelia and Charlie looked at each

other. "That is …"

Where to begin? *Could* they begin? What was allowed now?

"Allow me, old chaps," said a voice.

"Metti Rosby?" said Ms. Slaviero. "Don't tell me you're in on this too?"

"Afraid so, old girl."

Mr. Whitlock stood mute, but Ms. Slaviero was already figuring it out.

"Let me guess: you're *not* really my mentor from the Excellence in Teaching program, are you? And I don't suppose you really grew up in the city here, either."

"Ah, no," said Ms. Rosby. "At least, I'm not from the Department of Education. But I *have* lived on Earth since I was two."

"Oh, okay, then."

"Although that was only four years ago …"

"Ah."

Ms. Slaviero made a wry face and let Ms. Rosby

lead her away. Mr. Whitlock, looking dizzy, sat down on the sand and put his head between his knees.

Erik Zhang looked Charlie up and down. "How long have you known about all this, Floros?"

"Since Amelia got here."

Erik raised an eyebrow at Amelia, but his attention was on Charlie. "And you met this Krskn before?"

"Of course he did," Sophie T. piped up. "And that's nothing. You should have seen him single-handedly take on two giant alien ogres."

Charlie blushed pink, but all the kids looked at him with great interest.

"Not single-handed," he muttered. "Grawk did the hard work."

But if anything, Charlie being close friends with the vast alien hound only increased their admiration. Amelia smiled. Somehow she didn't think Charlie was going to be teased at school anymore.

Then her attention was taken by Mary helping a spindly man to his feet.

Leaf Man! Amelia thought, and hurried over to see if he was okay.

"I'm fine, I'm fine," he was reassuring Mary. "Embarrassed not to have been more help of course, but ..."

"Horatio!"

An old lady pushed through the clusters of people milling on the beach and held out her arms to Leaf Man. At first Amelia didn't recognize the crazy woman in hot-pink high-top sneakers, yoga pants, and a stretch top that read "Will Work For Chocolate," but of course, it was Matilda Swervingthorpe. Whatever had happened to her at Control headquarters, she'd obviously decided a change of wardrobe was in order.

"My dear friend," she was cooing over Leaf Man. "Are you quite yourself?"

"I'm fine, Tilly," he smiled. "Just happy to see you safe. I'm sorry it took me so long to find you."

Matilda shrugged off his apology. "Your timing was perfect, my dear Horatio. You know how I always wanted to see the future. And now I'm part of it!"

Leaf Man was grave. "There very nearly wasn't a future at all."

"Keeper!" called Dad. "Can you join us?"

They all went together because no one wanted to leave anyone else's side. Charlie jogged over, still blushing as his new fan club cheered behind him. Dad and Mum were standing with Lady Naomi, Arxish and another Control agent Amelia guessed was probably Stern, the mysterious third of the big three. James was standing to one side, trying to ignore Mr. Snavely, Ms. Rosby's slimy assistant. Tom was at the back of the group, his eyes fixed on Lady Naomi, not interested in anything else that was going on.

"Oh, Keeper," said Arxish. "Lady Naomi won't be frank with us, so we're hoping you will be a bit more helpful. Where do you think this canister and its substance have gone? Are they still a threat to gateway security?"

"What does Lady Naomi say?" Leaf Man asked quietly.

"I think it's been absorbed," said Lady Naomi. "I don't remember, but I think, or at least I feel as though it might, well ... be in *me* now."

Arxish rolled his eyes and addressed Leaf Man. "What's your assessment, Keeper? Is it possible? And if so, is Lady Naomi herself now a threat to the gateway?"

Leaf Man turned a lazy smile on Arxish. "Are you asking me if the person who saved us all should be treated like toxic waste?"

Arxish blustered. "Don't be so emotional. This isn't the time to worry about hurting people's feelings. I want to know: could the Guild use

Lady Naomi against us? Could they, I don't know, reverse the process and pull the wormhole back out of her?"

"You have the wormhole *inside* you?" gasped Charlie.

Lady Naomi frowned a smile at him. "I don't think that's how it works, but –"

"But she doesn't know," Arxish snapped. "You've already said so, which is why I want an expert opinion."

"I really think Lady Naomi is as much of an expert as anyone at this point," said Leaf Man, but he stepped cautiously towards her nonetheless. "Do you mind?"

"Not at all."

Lady Naomi stood where she was and everyone watched as Leaf Man slowly approached, his hand held out as if to a fire.

"Well?" said Arxish.

Leaf Man stepped closer and closer until he

was only three feet away. At last, he reached out and touched her shoulder.

"Nothing," he said. "Or, I should say, nothing you need to worry about. The power is there all right. I can feel it vibrating through her, but it's safe, somehow. Neutralized. Like the power of the gateway – opposite to the Nowhere, but not hostile to it. I don't think the Guild will ever be able to reach it now. It's been totally transformed."

Leaf Man looked at Lady Naomi, puzzled, but she turned away and faced Arxish. "There – I'm safe, and we've put the Guild off. Maybe not forever, but right now, what we need to worry about is *them*."

Arxish looked around and scowled at the humans on the beach. More and more people were coming down from the town and joining the throng on the sand. Parents, especially, were rushing to find their kids, and the crowd around Grawk was growing bigger. Amelia grinned to see him lying with his head between his paws, his eyes closed in bliss as forty or fifty hands all scratched his fur and fussed over him.

"It's unacceptable, sir," said Mr. Snavely. "Shall I call –"

"Thank you, Snavely," Arxish snapped. "I think I know how to shut down a breach of the Secrets Act."

"What?" said Ms. Rosby, just arriving with Ms. Slaviero. "Arxish, you're not seriously going to try to suppress this?"

"Of course not. But we must contain it until a special board meeting can be held to organize an investigation. We need to assemble a committee, establish the proper procedure for reclassifying Earth as a stellar planet, and then, after *that* has been ratified by the main office –"

"Oh, pants." Ms. Slaviero's voice cut across him. "Who died and made you emperor of Earth, anyway?"

"I beg your pardon!" Arxish began to turn purple.

"Apology accepted," Ms. Slaviero said briskly. She turned her back on him. "Look, as an Earthling myself, I think we humans can sort out for ourselves what happens next."

"Hear, hear!" said Dad.

"Yes!" Charlie shouted. "Finally! That's *exactly* what I've been saying."

"It's inevitable anyway," grumbled Tom.

"But you don't have the authority," Arxish tried again.

"What authority?" Ms. Slaviero glanced back at him. "From whom? Because I don't have any reason to respect *yours*."

Arxish glowered at Ms. Rosby. "Did you put her up to this?"

Ms. Rosby patted his hand. "I didn't need to. I've been trying to tell you this all along, old man. The humans can handle this for themselves."

"What are you going to do, Ms. Slaviero?" asked Amelia.

"Me, dear? Nothing. I still have no idea what is going on here at all, but I think *you* do." She looked at Lady Naomi.

Lady Naomi shied away and shook her head. "Oh, no – not me. But if you want someone to speak up, ask the Keeper."

"Well?" Ms. Slaviero asked Leaf Man.

"Keeper!" Arxish said, desperately. "Think about this!"

"I have," said Leaf Man, and followed after Ms. Slaviero.

She clapped her hands and yelled in her best bossy-teacher voice, "Round up, Forgotten Bay! Round up! Quickly, please!"

The people on the beach began to crowd around. They were only too pleased that someone seemed to know what she was doing.

"I have an announcement," she shouted, and

people all but ran to hear her. "Things have changed forever today. Not just here in Forgotten Bay, but for the whole planet."

Amelia saw people pull out their phones and relax as the screens lit up again. They were back online. Throughout the crowd, people began filming Ms. Slaviero.

"I don't understand much of what happened here just now," she went on, "but I know we were saved from certain disaster by friends we never knew we had. By the bravery of people who have been among us all this time, protecting us. They aren't quite who we thought they were, but we all need to be ready to understand. We need to show them that the human race is ready to be part of a bigger world."

She paused and considered the people in front of her. Many faces were confused, some skeptical, but almost all of them were curious and leaning in. She turned and pulled Leaf Man to the front.

"Your turn," she whispered.

Leaf Man bowed to her, and then to the audience of phone cameras. "My dear humanity," he said, and reached up to his neck. Pulling away his holo-emitter, he stood before them in his full, gorgeously, iridescently blue insectoid form. His antennae wiggled in the sunlight and he shrugged off his trench coat to spread his wings. Every part of him glittered, unmistakably alien. He held out his black, hooked claws to them all. "We have a lot to talk about."

Cerberus Jones

Cerberus Jones is the three-headed writing team made up of Chris Morphew, Rowan McAuley and David Harding.

Chris Morphew is *The Gateway's* story architect. Chris's experience writing adventures for *Zac Power* and heart-stopping twists for *The Phoenix Files* makes him the perfect man for the job!

Rowan McAuley is the team's chief writer. Before joining Cerberus Jones, Rowan wrote some of the most memorable stories and characters in the best-selling *Go Girl!* series.

David Harding's job is editing and continuity. He is also the man behind *Robert Irwin's Dinosaur Hunter* series, as well as several *RSPCA Animal Tales* titles.

THE GATEWAY

THE FOUR FINGERED MAN
Cerberus Jones

1

THE WARRIORS OF BRIN-HASK
Cerberus Jones

2

THE MIDNIGHT MERCENARY
Cerberus Jones

3

THE ANCIENT STARSHIP
Cerberus Jones

4

THE TIME SHIFTER
Cerberus Jones

5

THE DARK GIANTS
Cerberus Jones

6

THE LOST HOME WORLD
Cerberus Jones

7

THE LADY FROM NOWHERE
Cerberus Jones

✓